Jackie and Jesse and Joni and Jae

A Rosh Hashanah Story

by Chris Barash

illustrated by Christine Battuz

A Note from the Author

Every year, in the fall, people all over the world celebrate Rosh Hashanah, the Jewish New Year. It's a time to visit with family and friends. We eat special holiday foods, like apples dipped in honey and round challah speckled with raisins. Many people take part in synagogue services. It's also a time to think about mistakes we've made, to apologize to people we may have hurt, and to think about how we can each be our best self.

On Rosh Hashanah, many people go to an ocean or river or stream and throw pieces of bread into the water. This ceremony is called *tashlich*. We can see the breadcrumbs as our mistakes, floating away. Once they are gone, we can begin the New Year with a fresh start. Imagine you can toss away mistakes that you've made. What are they? How do you feel as you watch them disappear?

For my dear friend, Tracy Sherman—Chris
To my friend, Geneviève—Christine

Apples & Honey Press • An imprint of Behrman House • Millburn, New Jersey 07041
www.applesandhoneypress.com

Text copyright © 2019 by Chris Barash
Illustrations copyright © 2019 by Behrman House
ISBN 978-1-68115-550-0

Library of Congress Cataloging-in-Publication Data
Names: Barash, Chris, author. | Battuz, Christine, illustrator.
Title: Jackie and Jesse and Joni and Jae : a Rosh Hashanah story / by Chris
Barash ; illustrated by Christine Battuz.
Description: Millburn, New Jersey : Apples & Honey Press, an imprint of
Behrman House, [2019] | Summary: Four friends gather with others on Rosh
Hashanah for tashlich, when they apologize for mistakes they have made
then toss breadcrumbs on the water to represent the mistakes floating away.
Identifiers: LCCN 2018050081 | ISBN 9781681155500 (alk. paper)
Subjects: | CYAC: Stories in rhyme. | Tashlikh—Fiction. | Rosh
ha-Shanah—Fiction. | Forgiveness—Fiction. | Friendship—Fiction. |
Judaism—Customs and practices—Fiction.
Classification: LCC PZ8.3.B234344 Jac 2019 | DDC [E]--dc23 LC record available at https://lccn.loc.gov/2018050081

Design by Michelle Martinez • Edited by Dena Neusner
Printed in China • 1 3 5 7 9 8 6 4 2

Jackie and Jesse and Joni and Jae
walked down to the river one fine autumn day.

Neighbors and friends and the rabbi went too.
There was something called *tashlich* they needed to do.

It was late afternoon and a cool autumn breeze
blew leaves to the ground from the red maple trees.

Many who stood on the river's wide shore
had bags of stale bread—some held less, some held more.

Jackie asked Jesse, and Joni asked Jae,
"Is this bread for the ducks
or a game that we'll play?"

Just then Rabbi Miriam started to talk.
"It's such a great day for our holiday walk!

On Rosh Hashanah, we all need to say
'I'm sorry' to those whom we've
hurt in some way.

Now we come with our friends
to this colorful glade

with breadcrumbs that stand for
mistakes that we've made."

The four friends sat quietly there in the sun
and thought of some *unfriendly* things they had done.

Jackie knew Jesse
had really been hurt
last week when she laughed at the juice on his shirt.

She knew that was rude, and before very long
she said, "Jesse, I'm sorry.
My laughing was wrong."

Jesse remembered that one recent day
he felt angry at Joni for squishing his clay.

Then Jesse yelled loudly, but that wasn't right.
They both said, "I'm sorry. I don't want to fight."

Joni thought back to the time Jae had cried
when she roared from her treehouse,
"You can't come inside!"

She soon changed her mind and called,
"Don't go away!"
Then added, "I'm sorry.
Please come up and play!"

Jae had done something he knew that he shouldn't:
he shared Jackie's secret but told her he wouldn't.

The look on her face showed him Jackie felt bad,
so Jae said, "I'm sorry I made you so sad."

The four friends looked up
as they heard someone say,
". . . we're here at the river
for *tashlich* today.

Let's think of this bread
    as mistakes that we'll throw.
        Just toss them away.
            Let them sail! Let them go!"

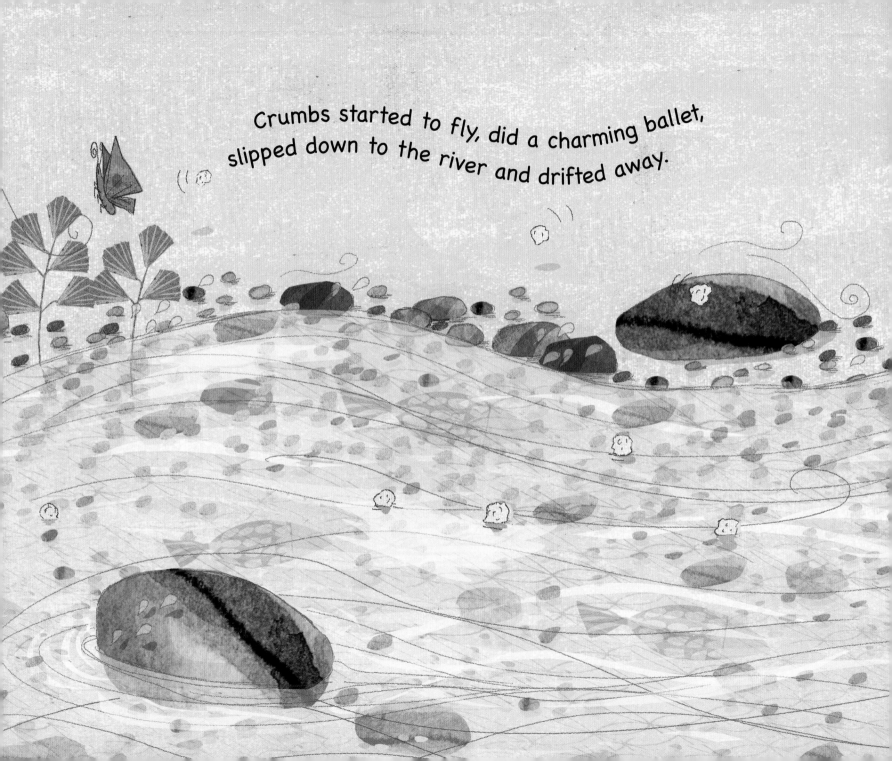

Crumbs started to fly, did a charming ballet,
slipped down to the river and drifted away.

Quietly, slowly, folks started to talk
and headed back home from their holiday walk.

Then Jackie hugged Jesse, and Joni hugged Jae.
They thought Rosh Hashanah was one awesome day.

Jackie said, "Next time I'll help you clean up
if juice accidentally spills from your cup."

Jesse decided to
make a fresh start.
"I'll try to stay calm
if you mess up my art."

Joni said, "Next time I'll make room for you. My treehouse is more fun when you're up there too."

And Jae said, "I really do want to you to see that keeping my promises matters to me."

Then Jackie and Jesse and Joni and Jae
walked home from the river that fine autumn day.